MW00989195

For my knitting girl

ISBN 978-0-988-324909
Library of Congress Control Number: 2012917587

Printed in the United States of America by Puritan Press
Published by NNK Press / PO Box 1635 / Atascadero, CA 93423

Copy editing by Nicole Crosby
Graphic design by Mary Joy Gumayagay

www.AnnieCanKnit.com

Annie and the Swiss Cheese Scarf

A new children's story about learning to knit

Written by Alana Dakos
Illustrated by Neesha Hudson

nnk
PRESS

Annie's mommy was a knitter.

2

At nighttime after dinner, Annie played with her dolls on the floor while her mommy sat on the big green sofa with piles of knitting in her lap. Even after Annie was tucked into bed, she could hear the click of her mommy's needles as she drifted off to sleep.

From the time Annie was a baby,
    she always had special knitted things from her mommy.

Baby booties and matching bonnets...

all sorts of hats,
    socks and scarves...

knitted dollies
    with knitted dolly dresses...

and even the special yellow baby blanket
that she secretly still slept with,
even though she was now big.

Annie was the only kid in her class
to have a special hand-knit sweater
to wear on the first day of school.

She felt so proud.

Annie loved her mommy's knitting. She loved the colors of the yarn and how it felt when she rubbed the bumpy stitches between her fingers. In fact, she loved her mommy's knitting so much that one day she decided she wanted to knit, too.

One night after dinner, Annie sat down next to her mommy on the big green sofa with her own ball of bright pink yarn.

"I want to knit a scarf!" she said.

"Well, let's first learn the stitches," said her mommy.

6

Annie's mommy covered Annie's hands with her own. She slowly helped her put loops on her needle and showed how to make the stitches. Annie watched each loop slip from one needle to the other as her mommy repeated a rhyme to help her remember what to do.

"In through the front door,

once around the back.

Peek through the window,

and off jumps Jack!"

Soon it was time for Annie to practice on her own, but her hands just wouldn't work right. Her fingers kept slipping and her needles kept falling out of the stitches. **"It's alright, keep trying. Just slow down and be patient,"** her mommy whispered as she helped Annie to fix her work. Annie could see how to make the stitches, but she didn't want to slow down and be patient. She had a scarf to finish! She wanted to knit *FAST*, just like her mommy.

As Annie sped up her stitching, loops began jumping off of Annie's needles and big ugly holes and knots appeared out of nowhere. Annie began to feel frustrated with her knitting. Her mommy made it look so easy. But knitting was much harder than it seemed. Annie's mommy tried to help. She said, "I had to practice a lot before I was able to knit quickly. Just take your time and before long, you'll get the hang of it."

Annie sighed. She didn't want to wait weeks... or days... or even hours. She wanted to be a fast knitter, and she wanted a bright pink scarf to wear to school.

Learning to Knit takes Patience and a lot of Practice!

And she wanted it now.

After a few rows, Annie jumped off of the couch and held up her knitting. This scarf didn't look like a scarf at all. It looked like a lopsided piece of

pink

Swiss

cheese.

Annie felt very disappointed about the whole thing. She didn't want to knit anymore.

Annie pouted and stomped off to her room where she shoved her knitting under the bed and nearly forgot about it altogether.

Until...

One day at school, Annie's teacher Mrs. Bee announced that there would be a class talent show the following week. All of the students would share one of their special talents with the rest of the class.

"Go home tonight and start thinking about what you are the best at. Everybody is good at something!" Mrs. Bee said.

Several days passed by. Annie couldn't stop thinking about the talent show and all of the kids in her class.

She knew that Emma could jump rope 100 times without stopping.

And Audrey could blow the biggest bubblegum bubble that anyone had ever seen.

David could hold his breath for an entire minute.

But what talent could she share?

She thought and thought.

She knew that she wasn't the best at singing or dancing. She never learned origami or cartwheels or how to play an instrument. She liked drawing pictures, but everyone knew that Luke was the best artist in the class.

It was the night before the
class talent show and Annie
lay in bed with her old yellow
knitted blanket trying to think
of an idea.

As she tossed and turned,
her blanket fell to the
floor. When she rolled
over to pick it up, she
noticed something
out of the corner of
her eye. Something
was peeking out
from under her bed.

It was long,

it was skinny,

and it was
bright pink.

17

Annie crouched down to get a closer look and pulled the dusty Swiss cheese scarf out from under her bed.

And then all of a sudden, she had an idea. She blew off the dust, picked up the needles, and she started again right where she left off.

She repeated the rhyme her mommy had taught her to remember what to do.

"In through the front door, once around the back.

Peek through the window, and off jumps Jack!"

But this time... she was slow and careful with her stitching.

She was shaky at first. She had to think hard to remember the right way to wrap the yarn. Sometimes the needles wouldn't cooperate and there were still some holes. But Annie kept trying... and trying... and trying.

As she practiced, her knitting looked less like Swiss cheese and more like a real scarf. Annie started to feel excited.

"Just maybe...
        this can be my talent!"
            she thought.

She knit and knit. The stitches became
easier and easier, and she knit faster and
faster. She knit until her fingers started
to hurt and until her eyes felt blurry.
She knit late into the night. When Annie
finally fell asleep, she continued to knit
in her dreams.

When Annie woke up the next morning, she felt tired. Her eyes were heavy and her fingers felt crooked and stiff. But she didn't care. She couldn't wait to tell her mommy about her new talent.

"Now we can knit together!" said Annie.

"I knew you could do it," said her mommy proudly.

23

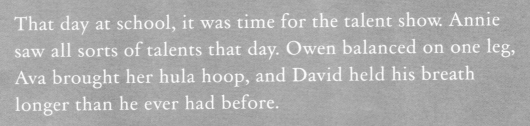

That day at school, it was time for the talent show. Annie saw all sorts of talents that day. Owen balanced on one leg, Ava brought her hula hoop, and David held his breath longer than he ever had before.

When it was Annie's turn to share her talent, she excitedly pulled out her scarf from her backpack and carefully unrolled her knitting for the class to see.

The class "oohed" and "aahed."

"Did you make that yourself?!" Mrs. Bee asked, surprised.

"Yes, I did," answered Annie proudly. "It took a lot of practice."

The students came up and felt her knitting.

"Can you teach me to knit, Annie, please?!" asked Emma.

"I love the color!" said Audrey.

"I like the holes at the bottom!" David said as he stuck his fingers through the bottom section of Annie's scarf. She decided that she wouldn't tell him that part was a mistake.

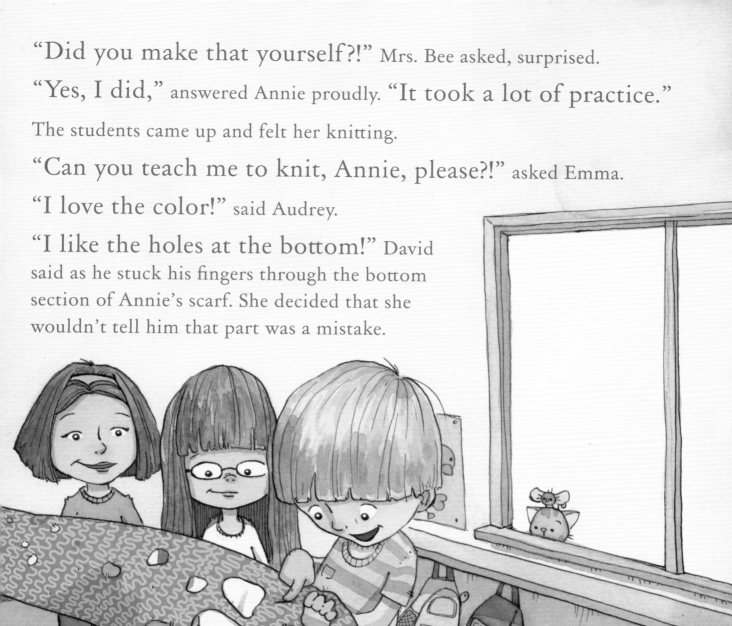

"I am so proud of you, Annie!" said Mrs. Bee. "That really took a lot of hard work and I am very impressed with your talent."

Annie felt very proud of herself, too.

Annie now spends her evenings knitting away on the green sofa with her mommy.

And she even teaches knitting lessons to her friends at recess.